Way To Go, Alex!

WRITTEN BY **Robin Pulver**

ILLUSTRATED BY **Elizabeth Wolf**

Albert Whitman & Company

Morton Grove, Illinois

~ Note ~

Way to Go, Alex! is the story of Carly's relationship with her older brother, Alex, who has mental retardation. Through her family's experiences with Special Olympics, Carly learns to focus on Alex's ability — not his disability — and comes to share in the joys of his achievements.

Founded in 1968 by Eunice Kennedy Shriver, Special Olympics has grown to include more than one million athletes in one hundred and sixty countries. Special Olympics athletes train daily and compete in more than sixteen thousand events worldwide each year. Athletes take part in twenty-five Olympic-type sports in local, state, regional, national, and world competitions.

The movement welcomes children and adults as well as their families and supporters. Hundreds of thousands of volunteers, corporate sponsors, and donors help the movement continue to grow and touch more lives of people like Alex.

—Dominick Egan and Chris Privett, Special Olympics

"Let me win. But if I cannot win,
let me be brave in the attempt."

— Special Olympics Oath

I'm waiting for my best friend, Annie, to come over.

But then Annie calls me up.

"Carly, guess what! Ryan scored the winning goal in soccer! Our whole family is going out for ice cream to celebrate. So I can't come."

I wish Annie wouldn't brag about Ryan so much. But I listen quietly. Dad says if you can't say something nice, don't say anything.

In Annie's family and my family, there's a mother and a father, a big brother, and a younger sister. You might think our families are pretty much alike. But they're not.

My brother Alex can't do things like other kids. He wants to, but his brain doesn't work right. Alex was born that way.

At school we were supposed to make up an invention. I drew a picture of a brain-fixing machine for Alex. It had earphones with message wires going to Alex's body. To his head, so he could learn to read and talk in whole sentences and say the alphabet. To his feet, so he could skip and pedal a bike. And to his hands, so he could stop scribbling and draw normal pictures.

I go to find Mom. "Annie's family is going out for ice cream because Ryan scored the winning goal in soccer." That's all I say. Not a word about Alex or what I sometimes wish.

Mom looks into my eyes. "Our family is different," she says. "But we still have lots to celebrate."

I suppose she's thinking about the time Alex learned to turn the knob and open the front door all by himself. He spent the whole day going outside and coming back in. He tracked mud all over the house. But Mom and Dad kept on cheering.

Now Mom says, "I have some news. I've signed your brother up for Special Olympics." She says Alex will enter the fifty-meter dash, the softball-throwing contest, and the standing long jump.

"But, Mom!" I say. "That sounds too hard!"

Mom says Alex's gym teacher at school will be his coach. Alex has eight weeks to get ready.

I worry that won't be enough. So I decide to practice every day with Alex. I want Alex to win something. But I am so afraid he can't win anything.

I draw a chalk line on the driveway to help Alex run straighter. Then we race each other, and I keep yelling, "Faster, Alex, faster!" Sometimes he stops and flops down on the pavement. I can't yell at him because then he gets mad and won't practice at all.

Next is the softball. Alex never throws it to me. Oh, well, what matters is how *far* he can throw it. Which isn't very far, I hate to say.

The standing long jump is a disaster. The only way I can get Alex to jump at all is to hold his hand. I say, "Okay, jump!" Then he just takes a big step and falls down on purpose. I show him how to do it, but he only laughs and does that big-step-fall-down jump again.

Mom brings out lemonade and tells us we are the two most wonderful children in the world. At dinner she brags about us to Dad. But how can she mean it?

What's so wonderful about big old Alex with his brain that doesn't work? What's so wonderful about me, who thinks things that aren't nice and thinks winning is so important?

On a sunny Saturday morning, we all head for the Special Olympics track and field meet. My stomach is doing flip-flops. Eight weeks took forever when I was waiting for my birthday. But eight weeks was not long enough at all to get Alex ready for this!

At the field, a band is playing. Alex joins other kids from his school for the Opening Ceremony parade. Lots of the kids look ordinary. There's no way to tell that they have learning problems. You'd have to get to know them, like I know Alex. All the faces I see are smiling in the sun.

A voice on the microphone calls for quiet. Then one of the athletes leads everybody in the oath of the Special Olympics athletes: "Let me win. But if I cannot win, let me be brave in the attempt."

Alex's first event is the fifty-meter dash. He lines up with two other runners. Only three runners altogether! Maybe Alex has a chance! I head for the finish line so Alex can see me there.

The starting gun goes off. "Alex, run!" I yell. He runs scrambly fast, like a scarecrow missing half its straw. The other runners come toward me, too. All I *see* is that look of happy trying on their faces.

Alex is in the lead. He's going to win! I am already thinking about calling up Annie. This is so great!

But then Alex stops. Right before the finish line, he just . . . stops.

"Alex! Come on!" He won't move. One runner runs past him and breaks through the ribbon. The other runner follows close behind. Finally, Alex crosses the finish line, too. Then I realize Alex didn't understand about the ribbon. *He thought the ribbon meant to stop right there.*

Alex is jumping up and down, he's so excited. We go right to the awards tent, where he gets a third-place medal.

It should have been first place. If only he had understood about the ribbon! Why didn't somebody warn him?

At the softball throw, Alex comes in third, too. Another medal! "Way to go, Alex!" I say.

But now I want to go home. "Please, Dad," I say. "Let's forget the standing long jump."

He says, no way, Alex is signed up for it; he'll do it.

When the moment comes to jump, Alex stands, staring at his feet. "Alex, jump!" I yell, but he doesn't jump. His eyes find me, and his arms reach out.

Without thinking, I rush over and take Alex's hand. "Okay, jump!" I say. Then Alex does his big-step-fall-down jump.

The official calls the names of two other contestants. Those two didn't come. Alex wins a participant medal in the standing long jump. All the people watching cheer wildly.

But I'm thinking, *We cheated*. Wasn't it cheating for me to hold Alex's hand? Alex was the only one. He didn't even really jump!

I ask the official about it.

"Hey," says the woman, "look around you. Alex made everybody happy by doing the best he could, by having the courage to try. And you helped."

Mom takes a picture of both of us. After that, our whole family goes out for ice cream.

"Next year," I tell Mom, "we'll practice with a ribbon across the driveway."

Mom's eyes are shining. I think she really does think her children are wonderful. Alex and me!

That evening, I go to Annie's. Ryan is building a humongous card castle. Suddenly it collapses.

"Dumb cards!" Ryan shouts, and stomps past me.

I want to tell Ryan to try again. Ask for help if you need it, and be brave in the attempt.

My brother Alex taught me that.

For Special Olympics athletes,
families, coaches, and volunteers
everywhere. — R. P.

To my children, Sophie and Tony.
— E. W.

Library of Congress Cataloging-in-Publication Data

Pulver, Robin.
Way to go, Alex! / by Robin Pulver ; illustrated by Elizabeth Wolf.
p. cm.
Summary: Carly learns a lot about Alex, her mentally disabled older brother,
as he trains for and competes in the Special Olympics. Includes a note from
the Special Olympics.
ISBN 0-8075-1583-3
[1. Mentally handicapped — Fiction.
2. Brothers and sisters — Fiction.
3. Special Olympics — Fiction.]
I. Wolf, Elizabeth, 1954–   ill.
II. Title.
PZ7.P973325Way   1999
[E] — dc21
99-10683
CIP

Text copyright © 1999 by Robin Pulver.
Illustrations copyright © 1999 by Elizabeth Wolf.
Published in 1999 by Albert Whitman & Company,
6340 Oakton Street, Morton Grove, Illinois, 60053-2723.
Published simultaneously in Canada by General Publishing, Limited, Toronto.
Printed in the United States of America.
10 9 8 7 6 5 4 3 2 1

The design is by Scott Piehl.